To Pash—gorgeous, charming spotty girl . . .
except for the snail-crunching!

GROSSET & DUNLAP
Published by the Penguin Group
Penguin Group (USA) Inc., 375 Hudson Street, New York, New York 10014, USA

USA | Canada | UK | Ireland | Australia | New Zealand | India | South Africa | China
Penguin Books Ltd, Registered Offices: 80 Strand, London WC2R 0RL, England

For more information about the Penguin Group visit penguin.com

Text copyright © 2009 Sue Bentley. Illustrations copyright © 2009 Angela Swan. Cover illustration © 2009 Andrew Farley. First printed in Great Britain in 2009 by Penguin Books Ltd. First published in the United States in 2013 by Grosset & Dunlap, a division of Penguin Young Readers Group, 345 Hudson Street, New York, New York 10014. GROSSET & DUNLAP is a trademark of Penguin Group (USA) Inc. Printed in the U.S.A.

Library of Congress Cataloging-in-Publication Data is available.

ISBN 978-0-448-46733-7   10 9 8 7 6 5 4 3 2 1

Friendship Forever

SUE BENTLEY

Illustrated by Angela Swan

Grosset & Dunlap
An Imprint of Penguin Group (USA) Inc.

Prologue

Storm padded slowly along the shore of the frozen lake. Snow clouds gathered in the sky above the young silver-gray wolf.

Suddenly, a piercing howl echoed in the frosty air.

"Shadow!" Storm gasped, trembling with fear.

The fierce lone wolf, who had

attacked the Moon-claw pack and left
Storm's mother injured, was close by.
Storm must disguise himself, and quickly!

There was a dazzling gold flash and a
fountain of golden sparks that reflected off
the icy surface of the lake. Where the wolf
cub had stood, there now crouched a rare
Akita puppy, with fluffy tan-and-cream
fur, pricked ears, and big midnight-blue
eyes.

Storm turned and raced toward some
ice-covered rocks. His little puppy heart
beat fast as his paws skidded, and he
tumbled over and over in his haste.

"Storm! In here!" called a deep,
velvety growl.

"Mother?" Storm whined, leaping to
his feet and plunging toward the shelter
of the ice cave. The she-wolf was lying

curled up just inside the entrance. In the dim light, the tiny puppy saw her lift her head and her golden eyes softened with affection. Storm's whole body wriggled and his tail twirled as he crept close and licked her muzzle in greeting.

Canista nuzzled her disguised cub's fluffy fur. "It is good to see you again, my son. But you have returned at a dangerous time. Shadow is searching for you. He wants to lead the Moon-claw pack."

Storm's midnight-blue eyes flared with sorrow and anger. "He has already killed my father and brothers. I will face Shadow and force him to leave our land!"

"Bravely said. But he is too strong for you, and I am still weak from his poisoned bite and cannot help you fight him. Go to the other world. Use this disguise to

hide. Return when your magic is stronger.
Then, together, we will fight Shadow."
Canista's head flopped back tiredly as she
finished speaking.

Storm nodded slowly. He did not want
to leave her, but he knew his mother was
right. He leaned forward and huffed out
a warm puppy breath, which glistened
with thousands of tiny sparks. The healing
mist whirled around Canista's wounded
paw and then sank into her fur, but before
Storm could complete the healing a
thunderous snarl sounded outside the cave.

Mighty paws with iron-hard claws
began scraping at the ice. "Go, Storm!
Save yourself," Canista growled urgently.

Storm threw one last glance at his
mother. His fluffy tan-and-cream fur
ignited with gold sparks. He whined softly

as he felt the power building inside him.
The golden light around him glowed
brightly. And grew brighter still . . .

Chapter
ONE

Tyra Carson shivered in the early morning chill, as the firefighter helped her and her mom climb out of the boat. Her dad was unloading their suitcases and dumping them on the road out of reach of the flood water. "Thank goodness Pam and Mark have offered to let us stay until our house is fixed up."

Tyra wrapped her arms around

herself, glad to be safely on dry land. She
was nervous meeting Pam and Mark
Baker, whom she hadn't seen for ages.
They were old college friends of her
parents and lived at the other end of town.
Tyra remembered that they had a daughter
named Rachel.

Tyra saw a car pull up at the top of the hill. It stopped and two people got out. "Here's Pam and Mark!" cried Mrs. Carson, waving.

"All right, folks. I'll leave you to it," the firefighter said cheerily, climbing back into the boat. He winked at Tyra. "You take care now, young lady."

Tyra managed a nervous smile. "I will. Thanks," she called, as he rowed away to rescue another family.

It had finally stopped raining, but the main road was under nearly three feet of water after the river had flooded over the bank. Tyra tried hard not to think of their house with its water-filled downstairs rooms and ruined furniture.

A man in a kayak paddled past. He had a cat in a pet carrier balanced on his lap.

Tyra grinned, feeling cheered by the sight.
Her mom saw her looking and smiled.
"That's one lucky kitten, isn't it?" She
linked arms with Tyra, and they trudged up
the steep hill together toward the Bakers'
car.

Pam Baker greeted them with hugs and
kind words. "You poor things! You must be
frozen. Let's get you up to the house!"

Her husband, Mark, helped load the
suitcases into the car before they set off.

After the short drive, Pam went up the front walkway and opened the house door. "I hope you'll treat this place as your home," she said kindly, ushering them inside.

"That goes for me too," said Mark. "And if there's anything you need, you only have to ask."

"Thanks. We really appreciate this," Tyra's dad said.

"What are friends for?" Pam said. "It must have been awful to wake up and find river water flooding into the house. Thank goodness the emergency services came so quickly."

"It was really scary," Tyra agreed. "I'm so glad we're here now."

"Me too," said Pam. "I'll cook some bacon and eggs and make a pot of tea.

Things always look brighter after some hot food. Maybe you'd like to take your things upstairs and get settled in? Mark will help, won't you?" she said to her husband.

"Sure thing," Mark said brightly. "Follow me, troops."

Tyra felt herself relaxing as she followed Mark and her mom and dad upstairs. She'd forgotten how nice the Bakers were.

"Where's Rachel?" Tyra's mom asked.

"She's just run down the road to say good-bye to one of her friends, who's going on vacation," Mark explained, opening bedroom doors. "She won't be long." After dumping the suitcases, he left Tyra and her parents to unpack and settle in.

Tyra had been put in a small back
bedroom. "Pam's made it very welcoming,
hasn't she?" her mom said, placing a pile
of clothes on the bed.

Tyra looked around. There were
colorful posters on the walls and a
bookcase piled with toys and games. The
striped pink comforter, pillowcases, and
matching curtains looked brand-new.

"It's really nice," Tyra agreed. She looked toward the suitcase, which was now almost empty. "Is Jemima in the other one?" Jemima was a gorgeous china doll with golden hair and a blue silk dress. She belonged to Shelly, Tyra's best friend, who had recently moved away. Tyra and Shelly had decided Tyra would look after Jemima, so that they had a good excuse for making sure that their moms and dads would let them meet up again.

Her mom frowned. "I'm not sure. Which one did you put her in?"

"Me? I thought *you* packed her!" Tyra exclaimed.

"Oh dear." Her mom looked puzzled. "I checked your bedroom, but Jemima wasn't on your bed. So I assumed you'd already packed her."

Tyra had a horrible sinking feeling.
"I think I might have left Jemima sitting
on the sofa when I went to bed! She'll be
ruined!"

"Well, it can't be helped now. We'll
have to search for her in a few days, once
the water's gone down."

"Shelly's going to be so upset with
me when she finds out. Maybe she won't
want to see me again now," Tyra said
miserably.

Mrs. Carson ruffled her daughter's
light brown hair and planted a kiss on
her head. "Of course she will. Shelly
will understand that it was an accident.
You didn't leave Jemima at the house on
purpose."

Tyra hoped that her mom was right.
Shelly adored Jemima, who was very old

and had belonged to her grandma.

After her mom finished putting
clothes away and went downstairs, Tyra
sank glumly on to the bed. She thought
of all the fun she and Shelly used to have.
A wave of loneliness washed over her,
and she wished that her best friend hadn't
moved so far away.

Suddenly, the bedroom door flew
open and a slim, dark-haired girl burst in.
"Oh, I forgot you were going to be in my
room!" she exclaimed.

"Hi . . . um, Rachel," Tyra said
distractedly.

"Hiya, Tyra! I was at the same party
as you a couple of weeks ago. It was fun,
wasn't it?" Rachel said with a bright smile.

Tyra frowned. She vaguely
remembered Rachel having been at a

party she'd gone to, but she'd been too busy having fun with Shelly to notice.

"We can get to know each other now that you're staying here," Rachel said.

"Yeah, I guess so," Tyra murmured, shrugging. But leaving Jemima behind in the flooded house had been the final straw. She felt too upset to make much effort to be friendly to someone she hardly knew. Rachel flushed and her smile wavered. "Don't sound so excited," she grumbled. "I've only totally changed my entire room

around for you! How long are you staying
here for, anyway? I don't want to be
camping out in our attic forever."

"I don't know. Until our house dries
out a bit, I expect," Tyra told her gloomily.
*If I had my way, we'd be out of here and back
home tomorrow*, she thought.

"Rachel?" Pam's cheerful voice called
up the stairs. "Did you tell Tyra that
breakfast's ready?"

"Yeah! We're just coming!" Rachel
answered. She turned to Tyra. "You heard
that, right?" she said, before flouncing out
and stomping downstairs.

Oh, great." Tyra breathed a heavy sigh.
Rachel obviously hated her for taking
over her bedroom and seemed to have
completely changed her mind about
wanting her to stay there. Tyra found

herself dreading the next few weeks.

She stood up, intending to go downstairs when a dazzling flash of bright golden light lit up the entire bedroom. Blinded for a moment, Tyra rubbed her eyes. When she could see again, she saw a tiny puppy with a round face, pointed ears, and the fluffiest tan-and-cream fur she had ever seen. It blinked at her with enormous midnight-blue eyes.

"Can you help me, please?" it woofed.

Chapter
TWO

Tyra gaped at the tiny puppy. Was this one of Rachel's toys? She thought Rachel might have been a bit too old for a talking toy.

"Hello. Aren't you gorgeous? I've never seen a puppy like you before. You're almost like a fluffy little teddy bear! Who do you belong to?" she wondered aloud.

The puppy's furry brow wrinkled in

a frown. "I do not belong to anyone. I am
Storm of the Moon-claw pack. What is
your name?"

Tyra did a double take. "You-you
really c-can talk!" she stuttered.

Storm nodded. Despite his tiny size
he didn't seem to be too scared of her. He
was looking up at her expectantly, with his
ears pricked, and Tyra realized that he was
waiting for her to reply.

"I'm Tyra. Tyra Carson. I'm staying
here with my mom and dad because our

house is flooded." She bent down and tried to make herself smaller so as not to alarm this amazing puppy. She still couldn't quite believe this was happening to her, and she didn't want Storm to run away.

Storm bowed his little round head. "I am honored to meet you, Tyra."

"Um . . . me too." Tyra blinked as she remembered something that Storm had just said. "What's the Moon-claw pack?"

"It is the wolf pack once led by my father and mother," Storm told her proudly in a gruff little bark. His big blue eyes lit up with anger. "Shadow, an evil lone wolf, killed my father and three litter brothers and wounded my mother. He wants to lead our pack, but the others will not follow him while I am alive."

"Hold on! Did you say *wolf*? But you're a tiny pu—"

"Stay back, please," Storm ordered, backing away.

As Tyra straightened up, there was another dazzling bright flash and the air fizzed with a cloud of gold sparks that drifted harmlessly around her and fell to the carpet.

"Oh!" Tyra rubbed her eyes, and when she could see again she noticed that the tiny fluffy tan-and-cream puppy was gone. In its place there stood a powerful young silver-gray wolf with thick fur and paws that seemed too big for its body. Its neck ruff gleamed with big golden sparkles, like yellow jewels. Tyra eyed the wolf's large sharp teeth and strong muscles. "Storm?"

"Yes, it is me, Tyra. I will not harm

you. Do not be afraid," Storm growled
softly.

But before Tyra had time to get used
to the amazing young wolf, there was a
final gold flash, and Storm reappeared as
a tiny tan-and-cream puppy. "Wow! You
really are a wolf!" Tyra exclaimed. "That's a
brilliant disguise!" Storm began to tremble
all over and his bushy little tail drooped.

"It will not save me if Shadow uses his magic to find me. I must hide. Will you help me?" he whined.

Tyra's heart went out to the terrified puppy. She picked Storm up and stroked his soft little head. His fur was softer than cotton wool and smelled of fresh air. "Of course I'll help. You can live with me in my bedroo—" She stopped as she remembered where she was. "Oh, I might not be allowed to keep you. I don't know how my parents' friends feel about pets. And I'm staying in Rachel's bedroom. Rachel's their daughter."

"I understand. Thank you for your kindness. I will find someone else who can help me," Storm woofed politely, wriggling to be put down.

"Hold on a minute," Tyra said, shifting

her grip, so that Storm settled in her arms
again. She wasn't ready to lose her new
friend that easily. Before he'd arrived, she'd
been feeling really miserable, especially
after Rachel had gotten upset and now
didn't seem to even want Tyra there.
"There must be something I can do. Let's
go and talk to my mom and dad. They
usually have good ideas. I can't wait to see
their faces when I tell them about you!"

Storm twisted around to look up at
her, his little face serious. "No, Tyra. You
cannot tell anyone my secret!" he warned.
"You must promise me!"

Tyra felt disappointed that she couldn't
share her news about the magical little
puppy, but if it would help to keep Storm
safe from his enemy, she was prepared to
keep his secret. "Okay. Cross my heart.

Your secret's safe with me. But I'm still not sure what to do about keeping you."

"Keeping who?" said her dad as he poked his head around the door. "I came to see where you'd got . . . Oh! Where on earth did that puppy come from?"

Tyra almost jumped out of her skin. She'd been so busy talking to Storm that she hadn't heard her dad coming up the stairs. It looked like her secret was out! She gulped and did some quick thinking. "I . . . um, found him just after we . . . er, got out of the boat," she fibbed. "Storm must have been swept away in the flood and now he's completely lost. *Which is true in a way*, she thought. She had a sudden brilliant idea. "I . . . I really wanted to look after him, especially since I'm missing Shelly so much and Jemima got

left behind. But I didn't think that you
and Mom would let me keep him. So
I . . . um, smuggled Storm in here, under
my coat," she said, looking up at him with
what she hoped was a convincingly guilty
expression.

Her dad raised his eyebrows. "Well,
you're certainly full of surprises, Tyra
Carson! I didn't notice you picking up

any soggy stray pup and stowing it away!"

"I know. I was superquick. Sorry. It was a little sneaky, wasn't it?" she said, chewing her lip.

"You can say that again!" Her dad sighed, but there was a twinkle in his eye. "I don't know what Pam and Mark are going to say about this. I suppose we'd better go downstairs and see."

"Storm's adorable, though, isn't he?" Tyra insisted. "Have you ever seen such a fluffy ball of fur? He's so soft. Why don't you stroke him and see?"

Her dad reached out and rubbed Storm under his chin. Storm wagged his bushy tail and leaned his head forward in enjoyment. Mr. Carson's face softened, and he smiled. "Storm's a really unusual pup, all right. I wonder what breed he is. And

I like his name. It really suits him."

"So will you ask Pam and Mark if
he can stay, for me?" Tyra said in her best
pleading voice. "I'll look after him, take
him for walks, and buy dog food with my
own money. And Storm can come home
with us, when our house is all dried out."

Her dad gave her a rueful grin.
"You've really fallen for that little puppy,
haven't you?"

Tyra nodded. "I already love him so
much!"

"Well, I suppose I could put in a good
word for you, but if Pam and Mark say no,
there'll be no arguments."

Chapter
THREE

"Of course you can keep him until someone comes to claim him," Pam said the moment Tyra finished explaining about Storm. "I don't mind at all. What about you, Mark?"

"It's fine by me. You're the boss!" Mark joked.

Tyra beamed at them both. "Thanks so much!" She wrapped her arms around

ddled his fluffy little body.

Storm gave a tiny delighted woof and leaned up to lick her nose with his warm pink tongue. "That is good! This is a safe place. I like it here."

Tyra stiffened. Storm had just spoken to her in front of everyone else!

She expected cries of wonder and astonishment from the grown-ups and Rachel, but nothing happened. Storm's

midnight-blue eyes glinted with mischief as he looked up at Tyra. "Only you can hear me speak," he yapped.

Tyra smiled affectionately at her new little friend. Storm was full of surprises. She wondered what else he could do.

Her mom bent down to stroke the tiny puppy's fluffy tan-and-cream fur. "Storm seems pleased about being able to stay. It's almost as if he understands every word we say!"

Tyra hid a smile. If only her mom knew how right she was!

Rachel had been silent up until now. Her dark hair had fallen forward to hide her face as she sat at the kitchen table eating some toast. "Don't bother to ask me, will you? No one cares what I think," she muttered, scowling.

Pam looked at her daughter in surprise. "But I thought you'd love the idea of having a puppy in the house. You're always asking if we can get a dog."

"Yeah! And I've never been allowed to have one!" Rachel complained. "So how come it's suddenly okay for Tyra?"

Tyra's mom looked embarrassed. "If this is going to be a problem, maybe we should just call the local shelter and take Storm there," she said quietly.

"No, we can't!" Tyra burst out. "I've already promised Storm that . . . I mean, I've promised myself that I'll take care of Storm. He *has* to stay with me!"

"Now, Tyra, be reasonable. Remember what I said? This isn't up to you," her dad warned gently.

Tyra swallowed. She made a big effort

to stay quiet in case she made things worse. But she hoped that her parents' friends wouldn't change their minds because of Rachel's objections.

But she didn't need to be worried. "Rachel, be fair." Pam shook her head slowly and reached out to ruffle her daughter's dark hair. "It'll be nice for Tyra to have a puppy for company while she's staying here. All this upheaval with the flood is very upsetting."

"I suppose so," Rachel admitted grudgingly. Tyra heaved a huge sigh of relief. Storm was staying! She turned to Rachel with a grateful smile, but the other girl was staring at the table again and didn't notice. Tyra could see that Rachel's face was bright red and her lips were pressed together in a thin line.

She tensed as she saw that the other
girl seemed furious. She might have given
in, but Rachel wasn't at all happy that Tyra
had been allowed to keep Storm.

Tyra avoided looking across the table
at Rachel as she quickly finished her
breakfast. Storm was lying next to her feet,
with his wet black nose resting between
his fluffy front paws.

"Thanks very much, Pam," Tyra said
politely. She got up and carried her plate

over to the sink and then turned to her dad. "Is it okay if I take Storm for a walk?" At the word *walk* Storm jumped to his feet, looking bright-eyed and wagging his creamy bushy tail.

"Of course it is. Storm looks pretty eager to go out," her dad replied.

"The old playground is nearby. We went there once, when you visited. Do you remember where it is?" asked Mark.

Tyra nodded.

Her dad fished in his pocket for some money. "Here you are. That should help you out until you get your allowance at the end of the week. Why don't you buy a few cans of dog food after your walk?"

"I will. Thanks, Dad." Tyra went into the hall with Storm at her heels. "See you later, everyone," she called.

"Bye!" called a chorus of voices.

Tyra noticed that Rachel didn't join in.

As soon as she and Storm were alone, Tyra breathed a sigh of relief. "Phew! I'm glad to get out of there. Did you see Rachel? She was giving me dirty looks all through breakfast."

Storm twisted his head around to look up at her with alert blue eyes. "Why would she do that?" he woofed curiously.

Tyra shrugged. "Probably because she's mad about not getting her own way. She was furious that I was allowed to keep you, because she's never been allowed to have a puppy. How come Rachel's so grumpy when her mom and dad are really nice?"

Storm blinked. "I did not think that Rachel looked angry. I thought she looked a little upset."

"Really?" Tyra asked. "Anyway, let's forget about her for now." She looked toward a side street. "I think we go down there and turn left to get to the playground."

Storm's furry little brow wrinkled in a frown. "What is a playground?"

"It's a big field with a playing field and a jungle gym and stuff. You can run around."

Storm's bright eyes sparkled. "My favorite thing!" he woofed happily. Tyra smiled at the little puppy's eagerness.

She and Storm walked to the end of the road and then turned onto a long tree-lined avenue. On one side, the row of houses stopped at the edge of a large open space. There was a small fenced-in area near the road, containing swings and a slide, and a flower bed with cheerful tulips and daffodils.

Ruff! Ruff! Storm kicked up his heels and took off across the grass.

Tyra watched him running around and sniffing all the exciting smells.

As she wandered along, enjoying the smell of fresh-cut grass, Storm skipped after her, his tail twirling happily. Tyra found a candy wrapper and crumpled

it up into a tight ball so she and Storm
could play a game of fetch.

Storm was panting hard, his little
pink tongue hanging out, by the time
they were wandering back along the path
toward the road.

"We'll go and buy you some food
now. I bet you're pretty hungry, aren't
you?" Tyra asked.

"Yes, I am!" Storm woofed happily.

As they walked by the playground, Tyra noticed two older boys messing around on the slide. One of them was tall and tough-looking, with a thin face and short sandy hair. He looked about fourteen. The other one was shorter and stocky with brown hair. As they spotted Tyra they nudged each other and stood up. "Uh-oh," Tyra said nervously, slowing her pace.

Chapter
FOUR

"Is something wrong, Tyra?" Storm yapped, pricking his ears.

Before Tyra could answer, one of the boys called to her. "My friend wants to have a look at your dog! Ed says he lost a dog that looks just like that."

Tyra's skin prickled with alarm as both boys got down from the slide and stood facing her. She hung back, trying to

decide whether or not to ignore them and
hurry past. But she knew that the older boys
could easily catch her up if they wanted to.

Tyra lifted her chin and tried to look
braver than she felt as she and Storm
went toward them. "I think you've made
a mistake," she said. Then she lowered her
voice to whisper: "I don't trust these boys.
Stay close to me, Storm."

Storm nodded, his midnight-blue eyes
narrowing warily.

The boy named Ed, wearing expensive
jeans and sneakers, stood waiting as Tyra
approached. He turned to Storm and
crouched down, slapping his thighs to
encourage Storm to jump up. "Come here,
boy. Come on . . . er, Buster!"

"His name's not Buster. It's Storm,"
Tyra said.

"Says you," Ed sneered. "What are you doing with *my* dog?"

Tyra's heart began to beat fast, but she held her ground. "He isn't yours. He's mine!"

Ed's thin face twisted in a grin. "Prove it! What breed is he then?" He glanced at his friend. "I bet she doesn't know, Dale."

Dale grinned at Ed.

Tyra realized that the boy was right.

She didn't know what breed Storm was.
What she *did* know was that there was no
way that these two bullies were getting
their hands on her tiny friend. She started
to try and walk around the boys in a wide
circle, but Ed dodged in front of her.

"Storm—I mean Buster—is a rare
Akita puppy. How would I know that, if
he didn't belong to me?" he said
triumphantly.

Tyra couldn't care less, but she wisely
kept silent.

"Ed knows a ton about dogs," Dale
informed her. "You'd better hand that
puppy over."

Tyra's mouth was dry. Both boys looked
strong and mean. "You're not taking Storm.
He doesn't belong to you, so there!" She
gulped. "Come on, Storm! We're leaving."

Ed moved again to stand in her way. "I don't think so," he drawled.

"You can't stop me!" Tyra tried to edge around Ed. "Run, Storm!" But Ed moved like lightning. Shoving Tyra aside, he reached down to grab the tiny puppy. "Oh!" Tyra gasped as she stumbled against the metal slide, banging her knee hard.

Storm yelped as Ed grasped him tightly around his middle and held him under one arm. Storm's dangling back

legs peddled frantically as he struggled to
get away. A soft growl rumbled in the tiny
puppy's throat and his big blue eyes lit up
with anger.

Tyra felt a faint, warm tingling
sensation down her spine, but she hardly
noticed it for the pain in her sore knee.
"You rotten bullies! Leave Storm alone!"
she screamed.

"Make me!" Ed crowed.

Dale looked uncomfortable. "Maybe
we should leave it, Ed," he said. "I think
that girl's hurt."

"She's just faking." Ed stopped and
then a look of astonishment crossed his
face. "What's happening?" he yelled,
gazing down at his hands in horror. They
swelled up until they looked like a pair of
inflated purple rubber gloves! "I must be

allergic to that dog's fur or something!"

Ed thrust Storm back at Tyra. "Here! You hold him!"

Tyra gathered Storm close, protectively, while trying to balance on one leg.

"Hey! What's going on?" called a girl's voice.

Tyra saw Rachel in the distance. She was frowning furiously as she started to run. "Why don't you leave and pick on someone your own size!" she shouted to Dale and Ed.

"Huh! Some people can't take a joke!" Ed said. "C'mon, Dale." The boys slouched off with Ed still flexing his purple swollen hands.

As Rachel drew nearer, Tyra's legs gave way, and she sank down on to the flat end of the slide. Now that the excitement was over, she felt sick and wobbly, and her knee was throbbing.

"Thank you for sticking up for me, Tyra. You were very brave," Storm barked gratefully, and then his fluffy little face creased in concern. "But you are hurt! I will make you better."

Time seemed to stand still. Tyra felt another warm tingling sensation down her spine, but this time it was much stronger. Bright gold sparks ignited in Storm's fluffy tan-and-cream fur and his pointed ears crackled and fizzed with electricity.

Storm rested a paw on her injured knee and a glittering golden mist flowed from it. As the sparkles swirled around her, forming a sort of magical bandage, Tyra felt the pain grow hot and increase for a moment and then drain away, as if it had never existed.

"Thanks, Storm. My knee's all better now." She smiled at her friend. "You certainly taught that horrible Ed a lesson! Those purple hands looked really awful!"

"The magic will not last long and his hands will not be harmed." Storm put his head on one side and showed his sharp little teeth in a doggy grin. "Did you say that we were going to buy some food?"

Tyra laughed. "I certainly did, and I think you deserve a treat, too. How about a yummy dog chew?"

Storm woofed and licked his lips. Seconds later, Rachel came running up as time returned to normal. "Dale and Ed go to my school. They're always in trouble. Are you okay, Tyra?" she puffed.

Tyra nodded. Rachel must not have been able to see the effects of the magic

Storm had just done. "I'm fine now,
thanks. I wish Shelly could have been
here with me. She can be pretty tough
sometimes. Those boys wouldn't have
dared to pick on me and Storm then."

Rachel's face fell. "I came to see if you
wanted me to show you where the store
is, but I guess you don't need *my* help."
She turned around and marched back
across the playground.

Tyra stared after her. Now what

was wrong? Rachel was so touchy. Tyra just couldn't figure her out. "Come on, Storm. Let's find the store," she said. Storm glanced over his shoulder at Rachel, his dewy eyes troubled, before he scampered after Tyra.

Back inside Pam and Mark's kitchen, Tyra poured dog food into a bowl. With an eager woof, Storm began chomping it up.

The warm room still smelled faintly of fried bacon and coffee. Her mom and dad were sitting at the table reading newspapers. The radio was on in the background.

"Did you and Storm have a good walk?" her mom asked, as Tyra sat down with them. "Rachel went to find you. Did you see her?"

"Yeah. We saw her, and then she went off by herself. I suppose she had something else to do," Tyra replied. She decided not to mention anything about the incident with Dale and Ed.

The local news came on the radio and they all stopped talking and listened. After the reporter finished speaking, Tyra's dad smiled. "It seems that the water level's falling fast. We'll be able to go back to the house soon and inspect the damage."

"Maybe we can find Jemima and bring her back here to give her a wash and a brush up," her mom added.

Tyra felt a guilty pang. Since Storm had arrived, she hadn't really missed Shelly. But at the mention of Jemima, she started worrying again about what her best friend was going to say about the lost doll.

Chapter
FIVE

"I think we'd better leave Storm here,"
Tyra's mom decided, a couple of days later.
"We can't have him paddling about in all
that mess and getting filthy."

They were borrowing Pam and
Mark's car to drive back to the house.
Tyra wasn't looking forward to seeing it
for the first time after the flood, but she
had explained about Jemima to Storm

and he had offered to help Tyra look for her.

"Storm will be fine here with us," said Pam. She smiled at Tyra. "I could ask Rachel to take him out for a walk when she gets back from school, if you like?"

"That would be okay," Storm woofed gently to Tyra.

Tyra was surprised that Storm didn't seem to mind Rachel, even though Tyra wasn't sure how to take her. One minute Rachel seemed friendly, and the next she was all prickly and sulky. It was very confusing.

Tyra decided that there was no way she was leaving Storm behind, but she couldn't see how she could take him with her. She bent down and pretended to tie her shoe. "What should I do? I really want you to come, too," she whispered to him.

Storm's big blue eyes were thoughtful. "Tell them that you are going upstairs to get something," he yapped.

"Okay." Tyra wasn't sure what he was planning, but she stood up and did as he asked. "I'll only be a minute. I'll meet you in the car," she called to her mom and dad, heading toward the stairs.

"Have you got a bag I could hide in?" Storm woofed as he ran up the stairs beside her.

"Oh, I get it! Good idea!" Tyra went into her bedroom and grabbed an empty shoulder bag she'd brought with her. She usually used it for schoolbooks, but her school was closed indefinitely because of the flood.

Tyra opened the bag and Storm

jumped inside. "You'll have to keep very quiet and stay out of sight. If Mom and Dad notice you, they'll make me leave you in the car," she warned.

Storm's little muzzle wrinkled in a grin. "Do not worry. I will use my magic, so that only you will be able to see and hear me."

"You can make yourself invisible? Cool! There's no problem then." She had another idea.

"I'll tell Pam that you're up here having a nap, then if Rachel comes looking for you when she gets home from school, we can always say that you were hiding or something."

Storm nodded. "That is good."

Tyra shouldered her bag, with her tiny friend inside, and went outside to the car.

Twenty minutes later, Tyra and Storm stood beside her mom and dad in the kitchen doorway of their house. Tyra was stunned. She had expected that everything would be soaked through, but she was unprepared for the thick layer of smelly mud that covered everything.

"This is dreadful!" her mom said sadly. "Everything's ruined. We're going to have to strip the entire kitchen and living room and start over."

"It could have been worse. At least we're all safe," Tyra's dad said soothingly, putting his arm around his wife.

They began discussing things like insurance and something called a *dehumidifier*, which would help to dry out the wet walls. Tyra decided to leave them to it. "Let's try and find Jemima," she whispered to Storm.

Storm nodded. He was invisibly sitting up with his front paws hooked over the edge of her bag.

Mud sloshed around Tyra's boots as she went into the sitting room. She picked her way around soggy books, cushions, and

other stuff on the floor. There was a musty
wet-furniture smell.

Storm peered around curiously as if he
couldn't imagine what the house looked
like before the flood.

Tyra had a sudden thought. "Could
you use your magic to make our house as
good as new?" she asked eagerly.

Storm blinked at her with serious
midnight-blue eyes. "Yes, I can do that
if you ask me to. But that would mean

giving myself away, and then I would have to leave."

"Oh no. Don't do that! I never want you to leave!" Tyra said hastily, wishing she hadn't said anything. She couldn't bear the idea of losing her friend. "Mom and Dad seem to be getting it all organized anyway. I'm sorry I even asked. Let's just try and find Jemima."

Storm nodded.

Tyra kept looking, but there was no sign of Shelly's doll. She was looking behind the wet chairs and sofa, when she spotted a scrap of pale blue material in the mud. She pounced on it and picked it up.

"It's Jemima's hair ribbon! She must be here somewhere," she told Storm.

The tiny puppy leaned forward and his little black nose twitched as he sniffed

Jemima's scent. "I will find her!" he
woofed.

"No! Don't jump down! It's too wet
and muddy in here," Tyra said.

Storm grinned. "My magic will
protect me." He leaped out of her bag,
trailing a fountain of golden sparks behind
him. *Squish!* Tyra saw that there was
something like a faint gold bubble starting
to form around Storm's body, legs, and
paws. *Splat!* It hardened into something
stretchy that changed shape with his
movements as he began sniffing around.
Storm scampered through the mud, but
his fluffy fur stayed clean and dry inside
the magical bubble.

"That's so amazing!" Tyra said,
laughing. Storm looked cute and weird at
the same time!

"What's amazing, honey?" asked her mom from the doorway.

"Um . . . the way the water's all disappeared. Where's it . . . er, gone? You'd never know it was like a swimming pool in here a couple of days ago," she babbled.

"I know," her mom agreed. "And, lucky for us, in a few weeks' time it'll seem as if the flood never happened. Any luck finding Jemima?"

"Not yet," Tyra said.

Out of the corner of her eye, she saw Storm digging around invisibly inside his glowing puppy-shaped bubble. She hid a smile, imagining the look on her mom's face if she could have seen him!

Tyra saw Storm heading for the open front door. "I'm going to look in the front garden. She might have gotten swept out there," she said, following him.

"Okay. But be careful where you're stepping," her mom instructed. "I'm just running upstairs to get a few more things to take back to Pam and Mark's."

Outside, Tyra picked her way around soggy plant pots and flattened flowers. She heard a muffled woof and looked over to see Storm scrabbling in a pile of mud. He gave a triumphant yap as he turned and bounded toward her. There was something in his mouth.

"Have you found—?" Tyra began,

but she broke off as she spotted the
bedraggled light-blue dress, the matted
golden hair, and the doll's arm that was
dangling at an odd angle.

Chapter
SIX

The following afternoon, Tyra was curled up on the sofa with Jemima on her lap and Storm snoozing beside her. It was a dismal gray day outside. Pam and Mark were at work and Tyra's mom and dad were in town, shopping for new furniture and kitchen equipment.

"Poor old Jemima. I thought you were lost forever," Tyra said. She turned to

Storm. "I'm so glad you found her. Thanks again."

"You are welcome." Storm opened one sleepy eye and yawned. Lifting his head, he watched curiously as Tyra picked up a brush and tried to untangle the doll's hair.

Tyra wasn't making much headway with the brush. Jemima's once-bright gold curls were dull and matted, and her light-blue eyes were wonky and didn't blink properly any more. Luckily, her dad had managed to reattach the loose arm.

Storm was just settling down again with his fluffy paws tucked beneath him, when Tyra heard the front door open and close. There was a thud as Rachel dumped her schoolbag in the hall. Rachel's school hadn't been affected by the flood as Tyra's had.

Storm jumped up, instantly alert. He
stared across the room and wagged his
tail as Rachel came in and walked toward
him.

Rachel grinned at the cute puppy
and stroked his soft little head. "Hello,
Storm! Nice to see you, too." She looked
sideways at Tyra. "Why are you sitting
there cuddling that old doll? It's a mess,"
she commented.

"As if I didn't know that!" Tyra said more sharply than she'd intended. "I don't want to think about what Shelly's going to say when she sees her."

Rachel rolled her eyes. "According to you, Shelly's practically perfect. So she'll be fine about it, won't she?" she said. She flicked her dark hair over a shoulder and left the room.

Tyra heard her running up the stairs. Tyra stared after her. "Did you hear that?" she said to Storm, folding her arms across her chest. "What's Rachel all upset about now?"

"I think that Rachel seems like a kind person," Storm woofed thoughtfully. "She gave up her bedroom for you. I wonder whether she would really like to be friends, but is not sure how to tell you."

"But I don't need another friend!"
Tyra exclaimed. "I've got Shelly and now
you. In fact, you're all I need!"

A serious expression crossed Storm's
little round face. "I will not always be here.
One day I must return to my home world
and lead the Moon-claw pack. Do you
understand that, Tyra?"

Tyra felt herself go cold. She couldn't
bear to think of losing her magical little
friend. "Yes . . . but that won't be for ages,
will it?" she asked, her voice catching.

"I will stay here as long as I can,"
Storm woofed.

"That's all right with me," Tyra said,
brightening. She gave him a cuddle.

But she couldn't help remembering
how lonely she had felt before Storm
arrived. *It might be nice to have another friend*

my own age, especially since Shelly will be living so far away, she thought wistfully.

On Saturday morning, Tyra woke to find lemon-colored sunlight pushing through the curtains. Storm was lying on his side, with all four legs stretched out. As Tyra reached over and began gently stroking his soft tan-and-cream fur, his tail thumped against the duvet. Tyra beamed at her tiny friend. "How about a walk before breakfast?" she suggested, throwing back the comforter.

Storm jumped down eagerly as she dressed quickly in jeans and a sweater. Tyra was going downstairs with Storm at her heels, when she heard voices from the kitchen.

"Have you made any plans for the

weekend?" Pam was asking Rachel.
"Why don't you and Tyra go for a bike
ride or have a game of tennis at the
playground."

"I don't think she's that interested in
doing stuff with me," Rachel said quietly.

"Still not getting along? I thought that
you two would be friends right away,"
Pam said. Her voice grew gentler. "Give
Tyra time. She's probably still upset about
the flooded house, and she's recently lost

her best friend. She's bound to come
around in time."

Rachel sighed heavily. "Oh well, I'll
just have to think of something to do on
my own, won't I?" Her voice grew louder
as she came into the hall.

Tyra whipped around and shot back
upstairs before Rachel saw her. She felt
slightly guilty for eavesdropping and didn't
want to get caught.

Storm followed her and then stood
beside her on the landing. "Is something
wrong, Tyra?"

Tyra nodded as she realized that she
had been too busy moping to notice that
Rachel was feeling left out. "I haven't
been very nice to Rachel, have I? I feel
bad about it. But I didn't mean to be
horrible. I'm not usually like that."

"I know that, Tyra," Storm woofed, his mouth crinkling in a smile. "If you were, I would not be your friend."

Tyra smiled fondly at him. "Thanks, Storm. I'm glad you understand. Do you think Rachel will give me another chance?"

Storm nodded, his tail twirling happily.

"How can I make up for being so grumpy?" she wondered aloud, and then suddenly an idea jumped into her head. "I know. How about if I ask *her* to play tennis with *me*? Oh no, I just remembered I can't. My racquet and tennis stuff is at our house . . ."

Storm's fluffy little round face lit up. "That is not a problem!"

Tyra felt a familiar tingling sensation down her spine as bright gold sparks glowed in his thick tan-and-cream fur. There was a whoosh of glitter that trickled down around Tyra in a sizzling cascade and tickled against her arms and legs.

Tyra looked down at herself. Her jeans were gone and she was wearing shorts, a white T-shirt and tennis shoes. She closed her fingers around the handle of her tennis racket.

"Wow! Thanks, Storm. You're brilliant!" she said, smiling.

The last spark had only just faded from Storm's pale fur when Rachel appeared at the bottom of the stairs. Her jaw dropped when she saw Tyra standing there in her tennis clothes. "What are you wearing that for?" she asked.

Tyra thought quickly. "I was just about to come and find you. I . . . um, heard your mom telling my mom that you liked tennis. I thought you might want to play a game. There are tennis courts on the playground, aren't there?" She swung the racquet about in a pretend volley, so that it made swishing noises in the air.

A grin spread across Rachel's face. "You bet! I'll go and get changed!"

Chapter
SEVEN

Tyra, Rachel, and Storm wandered back
across the playground later that afternoon.
Tyra felt hot and sweaty after an exciting
afternoon of tennis. Both girls were good
tennis players and were well matched, but
Rachel had finally won by two.

Storm was wandering around,
sniffing at things in the grass. He found
something smelly and interesting and

threw himself on to his back for a good roll. Picking himself up, he shook himself hard before racing after Tyra and Rachel.

Up ahead, Tyra suddenly spotted a group of teenage boys playing soccer. She felt a stir of unease as she recognized two of them: a tall, thin boy and a shorter, stocky boy with brown hair.

Rachel saw where she was looking. "Uh-oh! There's Dale and Ed again. What a pain. Just ignore them and walk straight past."

"I was going to," Tyra said. She didn't think that Ed would be stupid enough to pick on her again. Not after Storm had taught him a lesson by making his hands swell up and go purple.

But she remembered how she had hurt her knee when Ed had shoved her against the slide and couldn't help feeling nervous even being near the rough boys. Dale and Ed were both much bigger than her.

"Hey, Rachel!" Dale called out. "Do you and your friend need a puppy-walker?"

"Yeah! We'll come over and take Storm out for a walk sometime! We don't charge much," Ed joked.

The other boys with them laughed and made hooting noises.

"As if!" Rachel shouted, sticking her nose in the air.

Tyra swallowed hard, worried that the boys would carry out their threat. She just hoped that they didn't know where Rachel lived.

Growing bored, Dale and Ed turned back to their game. Relief washed through Tyra. She was glad when they reached the road and the teenage boys were just small shapes in the distance.

"Ready for our bike ride, then?" Mr. Carson said the following morning.

"Okay," Rachel said. She made a face at Tyra, who was sitting with Storm on her lap. "Dad's trying to stay in shape. I have to keep him company or he cheats and calls into the café for a cupcake."

"Me?" her dad said innocently.

Tyra laughed. "We won't be very long," Rachel said. "Will you be all right by yourself?"

I could never be bored with Storm around, Tyra thought. "I'll find something to do. No worries. Maybe I'll try to clean up Jemima again, although it's probably a waste of time," she said.

Rachel nodded and Tyra didn't see the thoughtful look on her face.

After she and Storm waved to Rachel and her dad as they cycled away, Tyra wandered back through the empty house.

Tyra's mom and dad were down at their house. Tyra hadn't wanted to go with them this time. It was too depressing to see the downstairs rooms, now stripped of all their furniture and carpets and looking horribly bare.

Pam was in the back garden. She looked up as Tyra and Storm came outside. "Why don't you keep me company?" she suggested. "I could use a hand."

"I don't mind," Tyra said, smiling.

She wasn't interested in gardening, but she thought Storm might enjoy running around in the fresh air, and she could leave the problem of Jemima until later.

"You could do some weeding, if you don't mind," Pam suggested. She gave Tyra an old pair of gardening gloves and then showed her a small plot with rows of cabbages and other vegetables. "It's mainly tufts of grass that you need to pull up," she explained.

"No problem. I can do that." Tyra

kneeled down and started to work. The
spring sunshine was warm on her back.
Birds flitted about busily gathering nesting
material and two lime-green brimstone
butterflies fluttered overhead in a spiral
dance.

Storm snuffled about, exploring the
long grass, and then came to sit beside
Tyra. He watched her working for a while,
before bouncing down on to his front
paws. *Grrr-ruff!* He invited her to play
with him.

When Tyra didn't respond, Storm
darted forward, scattering the pile of
weeds on the path beside her. Grasping
the cuff of her gardening glove in his
sharp puppy teeth, he laid back his ears
and tugged. *Grr-rufff!* he insisted.

"Hey! Stop it, you pest!" Tyra scolded,
laughing.

Pam laughed, too. "Storm's one
determined little puppy, isn't he?" she said,
reaching out to pet him. "You know, it's
really nice having him around the house."

"I thought you didn't like dogs that
much," Tyra said.

Pam looked surprised. "What makes
you say that?"

"Well, Rachel's not allowed to have a
dog, is she?"

"Oh, I see what you mean. I love dogs,

but with all of us out of the house all
day, it wouldn't be fair to have one," Pam
explained.

Tyra nodded in agreement. "No, it
wouldn't. But Rachel really likes Storm.
If she had a puppy of her own, we could
take them out for walks together."

"I'm glad that you and Rachel seem
to be getting along better now," Pam said,
smiling.

Tyra felt herself going red. She
nodded. "We didn't at first, but I think
that was probably my fault," she said
honestly.

Pam patted her arm. "Maybe—but it
takes two to argue. Rachel can be moody,
too, even though she's got a heart of gold."

Tyra nodded slowly. "That's what
Storm said . . . I mean, I could tell that

Storm liked Rachel as soon as he met her," she corrected hastily.

Luckily, Pam didn't seem to have noticed Tyra's slip-up. "You know, I've been thinking about going part-time at the office for a while now. I think you've just helped me make up my mind."

"Cool! So Rachel *could* have a puppy, couldn't she?" Tyra said eagerly.

Pam nodded. "But don't say anything about this to her. All right?"

"Okay!" Tyra agreed. She felt a tug on her jeans and glanced down to see that Storm was nibbling the hem. A giggle bubbled up from inside her. "Is it okay if I finish off now? I think Storm really needs a walk."

"Of course it is." Pam smiled. "Thanks for your help. Leave those weeds there to dry out. I'll dump them on the compost heap later."

Tyra stripped off her gardening gloves on her way toward the back door. Storm trotted along beside her. Tyra passed two bikes, which were leaning against the house wall. She went upstairs, intending to go to the bathroom to wash her hands.

As they reached her bedroom, Storm pricked up his ears. "There is someone inside," he woofed softly.

Tyra frowned, puzzled. She'd thought the house was empty, and then she remembered the bikes. Rachel and her dad must be back.

"I wonder why Rachel didn't come to find us," she whispered.

As she went into the room, she saw that Rachel was bending over Jemima. She

held the doll in one hand and reached for
the scissors with the other.

Tyra stared at her in shock. Her mind
went into fast forward. *It all suddenly made
sense.* Rachel was still jealous of Tyra's
friendship with Shelly and she was about
to take her anger out on Jemima!

Chapter
EIGHT

"No—don't! Give her to me!" Tyra cried. She snatched Jemima away before Rachel could attack the doll with her scissors.

Rachel frowned in puzzlement. "What's wrong?" she asked, and then her expression gradually changed as she realized what was happening. "You thought I was going to cut up Jemima's dress, didn't you? As if I'd ever be that mean. Thanks a lot!"

"What were you doing then?" Tyra demanded.

"It doesn't matter now," Rachel said bitterly. Her eyes glinted with tears. She got up and pushed past Tyra as she went out.

While Tyra stood there uncertainly, Storm jumped up on to the bed. He began sniffing the comforter and then gave a triumphant woof as he made a grab for some things that were hidden in the folds.

"I can't believe Rachel. I really thought we were starting to be friends," Tyra fumed, and then she frowned as Storm padded across the bed toward her with his mouth full of silky material and long trailing ribbons. "What have you got there?" she asked him.

Storm dropped the objects in front of her. Tyra saw that the "ribbon" was divided up into centimeters on one side and inches on the other.

"It's a tape measure. What would Rachel be doing with . . . ? Oh no." Tyra groaned as an awful thought occurred to her. She'd just made a huge mistake.

"I mentioned to Rachel that I was going to try and fix Jemima up. I think she was going to make something for Jemima to wear! Now I've really done it. Rachel will never speak to me again," she said miserably.

The next few days were very busy. Tyra didn't see much of Rachel during the day as Rachel was at school. And most evenings, she and Storm went to the house with her parents. The dehumidifiers had worked really well, and Tyra was happier being there as it was starting to look more normal.

On Friday evening, Tyra and Storm were returning to Pam and Mark's house after a visit to the pet store. Tyra stopped to shift her bag onto her other shoulder. It was full of cans of dog food and packets of treats, and it was heavy.

"I bet we'll be moving home soon. Rachel will probably be pleased to have her bedroom back," she said with a sigh, feeling sad about how things had turned out between them. "Anyway, Storm, you're going to love living there with me," she said, cheering up a bit.

"Storm? Did you hear what I said?" she asked, looking down at him when he didn't answer her.

But Storm had stopped dead. Suddenly he gave a whimper of terror and shot through the nearest front garden gate.

Tyra frowned, puzzled. What was going on? She ran into the garden after Storm and was just in time to see him squirming under a hedge. Tyra bent down and peered in to where he was hiding behind a leafy branch. He had his tail tucked between his legs and was trembling all over.

"Storm? What's wrong?" she asked worriedly.

"It's Shadow. He has found me," Storm whimpered. "He has used his magic to send some fierce dogs to find me. Here they come now!" Tyra heard a snapping and growling noise from the street. She crept back to peer around the gate and

saw a man approaching with two dogs. As
she noticed the dogs' fierce pale eyes and
extra-long teeth, she caught her breath.

Quickly ducking back inside the
garden, Tyra crouched out of sight as the
dogs drew closer. The man struggled to
get them under control and finally led
them away. The growling noises faded as
he and the dogs turned a corner.

"It's okay. You can come out now,"
Tyra told Storm with relief.

Storm crawled out slowly, his fluffy
little belly brushing the ground. But his
eyes were still troubled and Tyra saw that
he was shaking.

She swept him into her arms and
stroked him gently as they went back out
to the street. She could feel his tiny puppy
heart beating fast. "Those horrible dogs

are gone. You're safe now," she said.

Storm shook his head. "I will never be safe now that Shadow knows where I am. He will send other dogs after me. If they find me, I may have to leave suddenly—without saying good-bye."

Tyra felt a sharp pang as she knew that she would never be ready to lose him. "If that horrible Shadow gives up looking for you, you could live with me always!" she burst out.

"That is not possible," Storm yapped, his little face serious. "One day I must go back to my home world and lead the Moon-claw pack. Do you understand that, Tyra?"

Tyra nodded reluctantly, but she refused to think about that now. She just wanted to enjoy every single moment she had left with Storm.

Chapter
NINE

The weekend dawned bright and clear. Tyra was in a pretty good mood, considering that Rachel still wasn't speaking to her. At least, there had been no other signs of any fierce dogs, and Storm was back to his usual lively self.

Tyra, Storm, and her mom were wandering around the busy Saturday market, while Rachel and her parents

were at the mall. Tyra had brought Jemima
with her in her shoulder bag.

"I might find a stall selling dolls'
clothes, and I can buy Jemima a dress with
my allowance. Maybe then Shelly won't
be so mad with me for ruining her doll,"
she whispered to Storm.

Storm nodded.

Tyra's mom paused at a stall to buy some flowers for Pam. Tyra wandered past her. She really wished that things were better between her and Rachel, especially as it had been her own fault that they'd had another fight.

"Hey! Look at that cute toy puppy, Storm. It looks just like you!" Tyra said, as she spotted a nearby toy stall. It gave her an idea. She took her allowance from her jeans and quickly added it all up. "I might buy that for Rachel," she said quickly.

"I think that Rachel would like that very much," Storm yapped. "But will you still be able to buy a new dress for Jemima?"

Tyra shook her head. "No. I haven't got enough money for both. What should I do? Could your magic help me?" she asked hopefully.

Storm put his head to one side.
"Magic cannot solve everything. I think
that you must decide what to do yourself
this time," he woofed.

Tyra made a decision. "You're right.
Sorry, Shelly. Jemima will have to keep
her old dress for now," she said as she
reached for the cute toy puppy.

Storm wagged his tail approvingly.

As Tyra was paying, she noticed a
teenage boy in a red baseball cap looking
at cell-phone accessories on the next stall.
He seemed to turn away quickly so that
he had his back to her.

"That boy looks familiar. But I can't
remember where I've seen him before,"
she commented.

Storm glanced at the boy in the red
cap. "I do not recognize him either," he

yapped, with a doggy shrug.

Tyra forgot all about the boy as she walked away holding the toy.

The smell of frying onions and hot dogs filled the air. The market was getting busier. People of all ages, some with babies and others with dogs, filled the aisles between the stalls. Tyra started to worry that Storm would be stepped on. She bent down to pick him up. "You'll be safer if I carry you."

"Thank you, Tyra." Storm sniffed the toy puppy and leaned forward to lick its fake-fur ears.

Tyra giggled and playfully took hold of his little muzzle. "I don't think it needs a bath!"

As she turned around, she saw the boy in the red baseball cap again. He

was facing her, and Tyra felt a jolt as she
recognized his thin face.

It was Ed, without his friend Dale this
time, and he was staring right at Storm. A
chill ran through Tyra as the teenage boy
came toward her.

"Aren't you a bit old for dolls and
fluffy toys?" Ed scoffed, glancing at
Jemima, who was poking out of Tyra's
shoulder bag.

"What's it to you?" Tyra said in a shaky
voice.

She thought at first that Ed was going
to grab Storm, but he hesitated and
seemed to think better of it, obviously
remembering his supposed allergic
reaction to the puppy. Suddenly, Ed
swooped down and yanked Jemima out of
her bag.

"Hey! Give her back!" Tyra ordered.

"What's it worth?" Ed crowed, raising Jemima in the air and about to throw her down on to the hard ground.

"No! She's made of china!" Tyra yelled, reaching up for the doll that the tall boy was holding out of her reach. But someone rushed up from behind and snatched Jemima out of his hands.

It was Rachel. "Run, now!" she shouted to Tyra, already weaving away through the stalls toward the parking lot.

Tyra didn't need to be told twice. She raced after Rachel as if her feet had wings, and the two of them burst into peals of laughter at the sight of Ed scratching his head and staring after them.

She lost sight of Rachel for a moment and paused next to some big delivery

vans. Suddenly Storm yelped with terror.
Wriggling out of her arms, he jumped to
the ground and sped between the vans.
At the same time, Tyra saw dark shapes
prowling toward her. They raised their
heads and she saw their abnormally long
teeth and fierce pale eyes.

Her heart missed a beat. They were
here for Storm!

Tyra slid between the parked vans
after Storm. Suddenly, there was a bright
golden flash. Tyra blinked hard as her
sight cleared. Storm stood there as his
magnificent real self. The majestic young
wolf's silver-gray fur gleamed and his
midnight-blue eyes glowed like sapphires.
A she-wolf with a gentle, tired face stood
next to Storm.

And then Tyra knew that Storm was leaving her forever. She forced herself to be brave. "Go, Storm! Save yourself!" she cried, her voice breaking.

Storm raised a large silver paw in farewell. "You have been a good friend. Be of good heart," he said in a deep, velvety growl.

Tyra's eyes pricked with tears, and there was a deep ache in her chest. She was going to miss Storm terribly. "Good-bye, Storm. Take care. I'll never forget you," she whispered hoarsely.

There was a final dazzling flash and a large silent explosion of sparks that crackled harmlessly down around her like warm rain. Storm and his mother faded and were gone. Tyra heard a frustrated growl as the fierce dogs slinked away.

Tyra blinked back tears as she stood clutching the soft toy puppy. At least she'd had a chance to say good-bye to Storm. She knew that she'd always remember her wonderful magical friend and the exciting adventure they'd shared.

Rachel appeared around one of the vans, still clutching Jemima. "There you are!" she panted. "Jemima's fine—no thanks to Ed!"

"Thanks." Tyra took the doll and then held out the toy puppy. "I thought you might like this until you get a real one." *Which won't be too long now*, she thought happily, remembering her conversation in the garden with Pam.

"For me? Aw, thanks. It's gorgeous." Rachel's eyes softened as she cuddled the toy puppy.

"I'm sorry I've been such an idiot. Can we be friends?" Tyra asked.

Rachel nodded delightedly. "Yeah! For keeps this time?"

"You bet!" Tyra said. Although she'd just lost one special friend, she now had a brand-new one. And her heart lifted because she knew that Storm would be really pleased about it.

About the
AUTHOR

Sue Bentley's books for children often
include animals, fairies, and wildlife. She
lives in Northampton, England, and enjoys
reading, going to the cinema, relaxing
by her garden pond, and watching the
birds feeding their babies on the lawn.
At school she was always getting told off
for daydreaming or staring out of the
window—but she now realizes that she
was storing up ideas for when she became
a writer. She has met and owned many
cats and dogs, and each one has brought a
special kind of magic to her life.

Don't miss these Magic Ponies books!

Don't miss these Magic Kitten books!

Don't miss these Magic Puppy books!

Don't miss these Magic Bunny books!